Dedicated to the children of East Harlem and barrios
everywhere. — M.S.

For Deborah, an original. — Y.H. & C.V.W.

Published in the United States of America by Star Bright Books, Inc. The name
Star Bright Books and the Star Bright Books logo are registered trademarks of
Star Bright Books, Inc.

Please visit www.starbrightbooks.com. For orders, email:
orders@starbrightbooks.com, or call customer service at: (617) 354-1300.

Hardcover ISBN-13: 978-1-887734-85-1   Paperback ISBN-13: 978-1-932065-06-0
ISBN-10: 1-887734-85-6   ISBN-10: 1-932065-06-7
Star Bright Books / NY / 00209030   Star Bright Books / MA / 01007190
Printed in China 10 9 8 7 6 5 4 3 2   Printed in China / WKT / 15 14 13 12 11 10

Printed on paper from sustainable forests.

Library of Congress Cataloging-in-Publication Data

Starr, Meg.
  Alicia's happy day / by Meg Starr ; illustrated by Ying Hwa-hu and
Cornelius Van Wright.
      p. cm.
Summary: Alicia receives greetings from her Hispanic neighborhood as she
walks to her birthday party.
  ISBN 1-887734-85-6
[1. Birthdays–Fiction. 2. Parties–Fiction. 3. Hispanic
Americans–Fiction.] I. Hwa-hu, Ying, ill. II. Van Wright, Cornelius,
ill. III. Title.
  PZ7.S79735 Al 2002
  [E]–dc21
                            2001004142

ALICIA'S HAPPY DAY

By Meg Starr

Illustrated by

Ying-hwa Hu & Cornelius Van Wright

Star Bright Books
Cambridge Massachusetts

May you have a day
that's twirly-swirly.

May you hear salsa
and start to dance.

May the flags
all fly for you,

Taxicabs all stop for you,

Airplanes write in the sky for you,

Walk signs say "walk" in time for you,

And pigeons bow
shiny necks to you,

While friends
decorate in
chalk for you.

May the Orange lady give
a ribbon of peel to you,

And the Icey man say,
"Helado de Coco for you."

May Mammi
and Poppi hug
you,

Titi Penelope
sing to you,

Baby Anibal give
his bobo to you.

May you laugh as loud as you want, with no one to stop you, because all of us, we're all for you—that's why we sing happy birthday to YOU!